W9-CSJ-735

Tickle's Tale

Written by Stephen Cosgrove
Illustrated by Robin James

A Serendipity™ Book

PRICE STERN SLOAN
Los Angeles

The Serendipity™ Series was created by Stephen Cosgrove and Robin James.

Copyright © 1995, 1989 Price Stern Sloan, Inc.
Published by Price Stern Sloan, Inc.,
A member of The Putnam & Grosset Group, New York, New York.

Printed in the United States of America. Published simultaneously in Canada.
All rights reserved. No part of this publication may be reproduced, stored in a retrieval system
or transmitted, in any form or by any means, electronic, mechanical, photocopying, recording,
or otherwise, without the prior written permission of the publisher.

Library of Congress Catalog Card Number: 89-60565

ISBN 0-8431-3826-2

Serendipity™ and The Pink Dragon® are trademarks of Price Stern Sloan, Inc.

3 5 7 9 10 8 6 4 2

Dedicated to the memory of cats and
kittens (especially Jake and Charles Dickens),
for they all brought magic to me.

—*Stephen*

All in all, in the land of Serendipity, there was very little magic beyond your imagination. Even so, high in the crags and crannies of Mashew Peeshoo, near the crystal Lake of Mirrors, stood a small, stone castle where wondrous, magical things happened. Here, lightning flashed and crackled on crystal clear days and rainbows arched high above the walls of the castle keep. This was the castle of the Wizard Wink—master of illusion and magic.

The Wizard Wink was a kind and gentle wizard who actually read more than he whizzed his wizardry. He would sit for hours bathed in the golden light that streamed like ribbons through windows opened wide, reading books about this and that.

Around him, on dusty shelves and a rickety table, were powders and potions stored in vials and vases. There was purple plume powder, dream dust, feathered flames, and other such puffery much needed and used in the wizard trade.

Although he knew other wizards, Wink did not have any friends who slept over or even dropped by for tea, for they were just as reclusive as he.

Who he had instead, and who was a very good friend indeed, was a bright white cat called Tickle. He was called Tickle because he loved to tickle his own pink nose with his fluffy, fluffy tail as he ran around and around, trying to touch one to the other.

Tickle would tickle and turn, turn and tickle, until the tickles turned into sniggles, and the sniggles into giggles, and the giggles became gales of laughter.

Tickle had full run of the castle and he would prowl about as cats are wont to do. Sometimes he would look for scurrying mice that never seemed to be found. Mostly, he would spend his days on a shelf curled in a warm ray of sunshine. From his lofty perch, he would watch with a lazy eye as the Wizard Wink read from his book of magic and whisked and whipped his potent potions.

Now, the wizard didn't have many rules. But the rules he had were short and simple: sip your milk, don't slurp; and never, never touch the magic. Content with the fact that Tickle understood the rules, the wizard set out one day for the village and left the kitten all alone.

"Take care, my little fuzzy friend," said the Wizard Wink, as he put on his wizard's cap and coat. "I won't be long." With that he was out the castle door, as Tickle's tail whipped sassily about.

The one thing about cats that makes them almost magical, and slightly mysterious, is their curiosity. Of this trait, Tickle had tons.

Harrumm, Tickle thought, as he stretched and arched his back, I'm very curious to see if there is any milk in the dish. With that, he pussyfooted across the wizard's table and jumped to the floor below.

He wandered and wondered about the castle looking for his saucer, but look though he might, no dainty dish could be found.

"Harrumm," purred Tickle, as he rubbed his tickly tail around a ladder's rail, "curiously, when there is no milk there are always mice. Beyond milk, mice are nice—very nice indeed."

Off he ran to look about for a mighty mouse or many mice that might be skittering about.

Tickle looked here, Tickle looked there, but nowhere could he find any mice, or for that matter even one single mouse. He looked in the gnawed hole in the castle wall. He looked in the untripped trap in the dusty hall. He looked and looked, but look though he might, Tickle found nothing—nothing at all.

It was at this time that curiosity, tainted with a bit of hunger, got the best of Tickle, the wizard's cat. He happened to find himself on the rickety table looking about for something to eat. With Tickle's tail idly twitching, he sat there in a pool of light on the wizard's book of magic delight.

Tickle looked around and then he looked down. It was then that he saw the most curious words indeed:

"If hungry you are, if starvation you fear,
say these words and food will appear:
Hocus pocus and lavender locust,
brighten my eyes, bring dinner into focus."

Below these words was an ominous warning:

"Don't use this magic more times than two,
though hungry indeed or curious are you!"

Curiosity will always get the cat and Tickle was no exception. Quickly, he purred the words out loud while thinking of gallons and gallons of milk. At first nothing happened, but then the skies turned purple and crickled and crackled, as lightning flashed and thunder crashed.

When all became light again, Tickle looked about for his magic meal, but there was nothing there: no saucer, no milk. The floor was bare. Beyond his sight, through the window bright, the crystal Lake of Mirrors turned milky white, but the cat just didn't see.

"Harrumm," he purred, as cats often do, "maybe I should try it again."

With his eyes scrunched tight, he meowed the words until they echoed all through the castle. This time, as he chanted, he thought and thought of the largest mouse he could. Once again, the skies flashed with lightning and crashed with thunderous roars. But still nothing happened. Nothing happened at all.

Nothing happened, that is, save for just out of Tickle's sight, a mouse the size of a house rushed from the castle and galloped into the meadow beyond.

Now, the warning was still on the page:

> *"Don't use this magic more times than two,*
> *though hungry indeed or curious are you!"*

But as we all know, cats rarely read something more than once, and Tickle's curiosity was tainted.

Without thinking of the consequences, he chanted the magical words once again:

> *"Hocus pocus lavender locust,*
> *brighten my eyes, bring dinner into focus."*

But this time, the third time, there was no thunder, no lightning. This time, the third time, there was only a puff of purple dust and a special spark that settled scarily about the cat. Tickle didn't have time to worry or wonder at this odd event, for out the window he spied the Wizard Wink wandering up the path and back to the castle keep.

Tickle looked about to make sure that all was in order, then he leaped to the shelf where he always slept. There, he plopped himself down and pretended to be asleep—and just in time— as the wizard waltzed in the door carrying a polished pine pitcher, and nothing more.

The wizard shook his head curiously as he scratched his long, white beard. "Hmm," said the Wizard Wink, "all of this is a bit odd. The Lake of Mirrors has turned into milk and cream, and I was passed on the road by a mouse the size of a house. Whose magic could this be?"

The Wizard Wink looked and looked, but nothing seemed to be amiss. The vials and vases were where they should be, and the magical book was open just as he had left it.

"Harumph," grumbled he, as he shook his head, "all this must be just an old man's imagination."

With one eye cracked open and the other asleep, Tickle watched and waited, but nothing happened. Nothing happened at all.

The wizard busily bustled about as he whistled a tune and poured some milk from the pitcher into a dainty dish. Once filled, he put it on the floor.

"There, my little kitten," he said, as he stroked the cat. "I knew you must be hungry, so I slipped into the village and bought you a pitcher of milk." Without further ado, the wizard went back to work and Tickle lapped at his dinner, delighted with his deception. Ah, yes, he was very relieved that he didn't get caught.

CURIOSITY CAN'T BE BOUGHT,

WHAT THEY SAY IS TRUE.

WHEN WRONG YOU'LL

ALWAYS GET CAUGHT, NOT BY HIM,

OR THEM, BUT . . . BY YOU!

Although this curious cat weaved and deceived, doing what was very wrong, Tickle never did get caught, but he now has a tail three feet long.

Yes, Tickle's tail is much too long, he can no longer play, and everywhere that Tickle goes, his tail gets in the way.

Serendipity™ Books

Created by
Stephen Cosgrove and Robin James

Enjoy all the delightful books in the Serendipity™ Series:

The above books, and many others, can be bought wherever books are sold.

PRICE STERN SLOAN
Los Angeles